Beyond the River

Beyond the River

Schiffer Publishing Ltd

4880 Lower Valley Road Atglen, Pennsylvania 19310

Alex Miller
Caroline Miller, Illustrator

Other Schiffer Books on Related Subjects:
Jemma's Got the Travel Bug. Susan Glick. ISBN: 9780764336324. $14.99

Library of Congress Control Number: 2010940966

Cover designed by: Bruce Waters
Type set in Humanist 521 BT

ISBN: 978-0-7643-3741-3
Printed in China

Schiffer Books are available at special discounts for bulk purchases for sales promotions or premiums. Special editions, including personalized covers, corporate imprints, and excerpts can be created in large quantities for special needs. For more information contact the publisher:

Published by Schiffer Publishing Ltd.
4880 Lower Valley Road
Atglen, PA 19310
Phone: (610) 593-1777; Fax: (610) 593-2002
E-mail: Info@schifferbooks.com

For the largest selection of fine reference books on this and related subjects, please visit our web site at **www.schifferbooks.com**
We are always looking for people to write books on new and related subjects. If you have an idea for a book please contact us at the above address.
This book may be purchased from the publisher.
Include $5.00 for shipping.
Please try your bookstore first.

You may write for a free catalog.
In Europe, Schiffer books are distributed by
Bushwood Books
6 Marksbury Ave.
Kew Gardens
Surrey TW9 4JF England
Phone: 44 (0) 20 8392 8585; Fax: 44 (0) 20 8392 9876
E-mail: info@bushwoodbooks.co.uk
Website: www.bushwoodbooks.co.uk

Dedication

This book is dedicated to Lucia Worthington and all others who have the courage to chase their dreams.

Once upon a time there was a little fish.

He lived in a calm little pond with a stream that connected to a river. The river was always filled with life and promise.

The little fish loved to go to the river and watch all the other fish. The bigger fish—especially the salmon—fascinated him.

Every year he liked to watch them swim up the river into a world unknown to him. He always wondered where the salmon swam to and what they did when they got there.

Time passed. The little fish grew older. The pond grew smaller. Some of the other fish started families of their own, beginning a new life in the pond.

But the little fish wasn't content. His mind still followed the salmon on their mysterious yearly passing.

When the little fish saw the salmon again he stopped one of them to ask where they were going. To his surprise, the salmon answered:

"We don't know. The river is endless. No one has ever made it to the end."
"Then why do you do it?" asked the little fish.

Now the salmon looked surprised.

"To find out, of course! Ask yourself this: is it better to live a life of safety, a life where you wake up wondering: what would have happened if I had tried? If I had given everything, would I have succeeded?"

"But what if you get lost along the way?"

"So far everyone has. But that doesn't mean it can't be done. When you can look at yourself at the end of your life and say:

Yes, I did all I could. I fought hard and gave it everything I had in me.

That is the way we live. Chasing a dream gives a special joy to life that can only be understood by the true adventurers who seek it.

That day the little fish left his safe little pond and entered into the world he had once only watched from afar.

At first he was scared. So many other fish were in the river; many were much bigger than him.

The little fish kept swimming. Time passed. Then something began to change. The little fish began to grow. Soon he was one of the biggest fish in the river.

He kept swimming, and the current grew stronger. He noticed that the farther he swam the fewer fish he saw. Soon there were only a few left.

The current was now very powerful, and each flip of his tail was harder than before.

But he closed his eyes and swam on... and on... and on.

When he opened his eyes he was the only
fish left. The current was now so powerful
he could not feel his fins. He glanced up and
down the river and was shocked!

All around him the water had turned frothy and white. Try as he might, he could no longer even see his fins in front of him! The current tossed him about, backwards and forwards, side to side. Pebbles and mud flew at him from all directions while water poured down on top of him. Slowly, he began to notice he was sinking.

"If my journey is to end here," he said,
"I won't give up without a fight!"

With his last bit of strength, he closed his eyes and flipped his tail with all his might. On and on and on until...

He opened his eyes. The terrible current was gone; an endless body of water stretched ahead of him. Out of the depths he heard the gentle voice of the salmon:

"You, my friend, have truly lived the adventure. While you could have spent your life under the shelter of a rock, you chose the path of uncertainty. By chasing your dream you now share that special joy known only by true adventurers. After all, a true hero is not the first to succeed, just the last to stop trying."

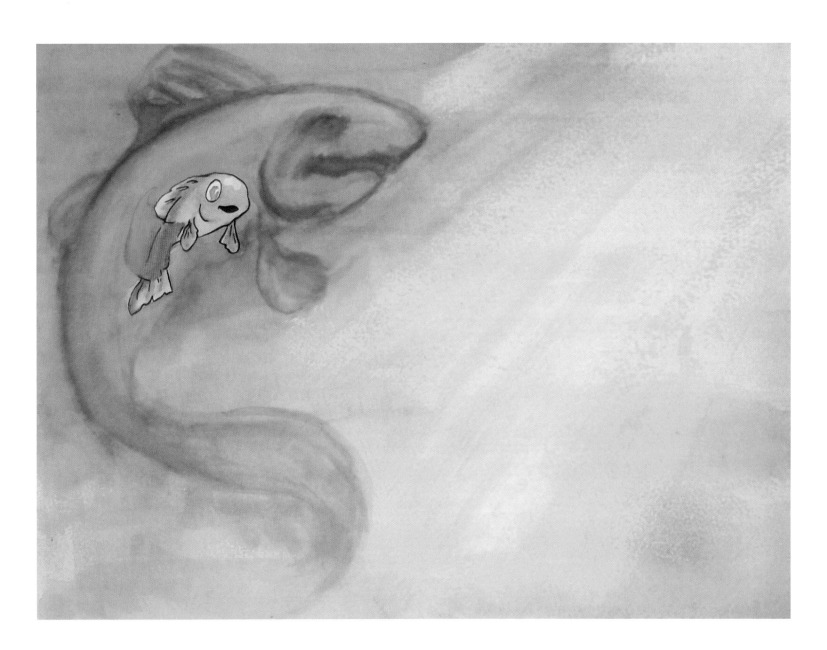

Suddenly, the little fish no longer felt tired. The frothy white water of the river had been transformed into a deep blue lake.

As he swam off into the distance, a ray of light shone down upon his now calm face… which, as it disappeared into the blue, revealed a triumphant and unmistakable smile.

And last, the little fish was happy.

About the Author

Alex Miller graduated from the University of California, Santa Cruz, and is also the author of *California Theme Parks*. He works for The Walt Disney Company in Glendale, California. Alex is also an avid swimmer.

About the Illustrator

This is the second book Caroline Miller has illustrated. She is currently attending film school at Virginia Commonwealth University. She enjoys painting, filmmaking, and animation.

More Schiffer Titles

Chickadee & The Whale: A Baby Chickadee's Adventure. Catherine E. Clark. A charming story about a baby songbird, Chickadee, and baby Humpback Whale, who befriends the small songbird when he wanders away from the safety of the forest and finds himself in danger over the open ocean. They become friends and after the storm ends the baby whale and his mom take Chickadee back to land and to his family.
Their story introduces a variety of real wildlife in the forest, on the beach, and in the ocean, with wonderful artwork and detail, and is told in a way that will delight and educate. Grades 1-3.

Size: 11" x 8 1/2"   40 full color illustrations   40 pp.
ISBN: 978-0-7643-2950-0   hard cover $16.95

Mother Monarch. Mindy Lighthipe. 23 colorful illustrations and a friendly text tell the story of the Monarch butterfly's lifecycle from the mother laying eggs, to a hatching caterpillar, to pupating into a chrysalis, and a new generation and its amazing migration South. An important link is emphasized between the Monarch butterfly and the host plant, the Common Milkweed. Ages 4-10 years.

Size: 11" x 8 1/2"   23 color illustrations   32 pp.
ISBN: 978-0-7643-3400-9   hard cover $19.99

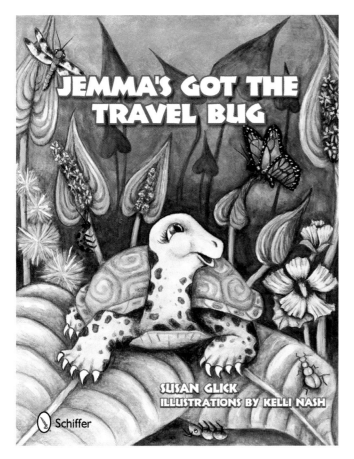

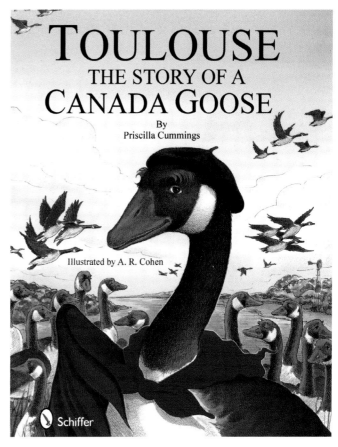

Jemma's Got the Travel Bug. Susan Glick.
Illustrations by Kelli Nash. Jemma, a young
diamondback terrapin, leaves her quiet cove and
ventures into the open waters of the Chesapeake
Bay. Away from home, she encounters the dangers
that threaten the diamondback terrapin. This
illustrated, action-filled story is perfect for children
in grades K-5.

Size: 8 1/2" x 11"   16 illustrations   32 pp.
ISBN: 978-0-7643-3632-4   hard cover $14.99

Toulouse: The Story of a Canada Goose.
Priscilla Cummings. Illustrated by A. R. Cohen.
One October day a young Canada goose became
separated from his family on his first migration
south. He and a lost snow goose became special
friends for life. Their love story will be treasured
by children and adults alike. Preschool to grade 2

Size: 7' x 10"   19 color illustrations   30 pp.
ISBN: 978-0-7643-3692-8   hard cover $9.95

Beddy Bye in the Bay. Priscilla Cummings. Illustrations by Marcy Dunn Ramsey. The creatures of the Chesapeake Bay come to life in this delightful, informative story about how and where they sleep. Herons, crabs, clams, turtles, and fish each find a different place to rest in the water and along the shore. Ducks, butterflies, birds, beavers, and even oysters sleep in their own "beds." Once heard, this charming poem will be asked for every night. Beddy bye! Ages 6 and under.

Size: 8 1/8" x 9 1/8"	32 color illustration	32 pp.
ISBN: 978-0-7643-3450-4	hard cover	$14.99

Schiffer books may be ordered from your local bookstore, or they may be ordered directly from the publisher by writing to:
Schiffer Publishing, Ltd.
4880 Lower Valley Rd.
Atglen, PA 19310
(610) 593-1777; Fax (610) 593-2002
E-mail: Info@schifferbooks.com

Please visit our web site catalog at *www.schifferbooks.com* or write for a free catalog. Please include $5.00 for shipping and handling for the first two books and $2.00 for each additional book. Full-price orders over $150 are shipped free in the U.S.

Printed in the China